MAGIC CARD tricks

Author: Kris Hirschmann
Designer: Deena Fleming

Scholastic and Tangerine Press and associated logos are trademarks of Scholastic Inc.
Published by Tangerine Press, an imprint of Scholastic Inc.,
557 Broadway; New York, NY 10012

Scholastic Canada
Markham, Ontario

Scholastic Australia
Gosford NSW

10 9 8 7 6 5 4 3 2 1

ISBN 0-439-85308-7
Printed and bound in China

CONTENTS

SO YOU WANT TO BE A MAGICIAN!

If you want to learn magic, card tricks are a great place to start. WHY? There are a bunch of reasons. For one thing, you don't need a lot of equipment. Also, many card tricks are simple to learn, and they work almost every time.

Wait a second. What was that last thing? Are we implying that magic tricks FAIL sometimes? OH, YES. It's a sad but true part of being a magician. You can increase your chances of success, however, by choosing tricks that are more-or-less foolproof—and that's EXACTLY what we have done in this book. The 28 tricks on the following pages are easy to learn and easy to perform. They are also VERY HARD to flub (magician-speak for goofing up).

So we've done our part. The rest is up to you. Read the tricks and practice them. MEMORIZE them, even. Then get ready to RAZZLE-DAZZLE your friends and family. After reading this book, you'll never look at a deck of playing cards the same way again!

MAGIC TERMS

You'll need to know a couple of basic magic terms to understand the instructions in this book. Let's review, shall we?

Faceup
The card's picture side is visible.

Facedown
The card's back side is visible.

Fan
Spread the cards apart.

Cut
Separate the deck into two parts.

Square the Deck
Tap or squeeze the cards until the edges of the deck are smooth.

Complete Cut
Separate the deck, then move the pile that was originally on the top of the deck to the bottom.

Top of the Deck
The upward side of the deck.

Bottom of the Deck
The downward side of the deck.

Overhand Shuffle
Pull a packet of cards from the bottom of the deck. Drop them a few at a time onto the top of the deck until the packet is gone. In this book, the term shuffle always means overhand shuffle.

OTHER MUST KNOW MAGIC STUFF

Here are a few more things you should know. HEED THESE BITS OF ADVICE if you want to perform the tricks in this book as well as possible.

Tools of the Trade

This book comes with two decks of cards. The red deck is a regular deck. It is used for the tricks in Sections 1 through 5. The blue deck is tapered. It is used for the tricks in Section 6.

BRAIN POWER

Each trick is rated one, two, or three brains. One-brainers are super-easy to learn and need little or no setup. Two-brainers take a little more effort. Three-brainers are the hardest of all—but they also tend to be the most spectacular, so they're worth the effort.

SET THE STAGE

Follow the instructions in this section, if any, BEFORE your show. These are SECRET STEPS that the audience must not see.

PATTER PROMPTER

Have you ever noticed that magicians usually talk nonstop while they're performing? There's a reason for this. It distracts the audience from any SNEAKY MOVES they may be doing. Magicians' talk is called patter, and it provides a storyline for a trick. The Patter Prompter section gives you one story idea. Remember, THIS IS JUST A START. You'll have to flesh out the concept on your own.

No Peeking

Unless the instructions say otherwise, you should NEVER SEE a card chosen by a volunteer. Close your eyes, turn your back, or do whatever else it takes to convince your volunteer that you are completely, totally, 100% INNOCENT. (Yeah, right.)

7

SECTION

1: KEY CARD TRICKS

In magic jargon, a key card is a known card that is forced to end up next to an unknown card. When the magician finds the key card, he or she finds the unknown card as well. ABRACADABRA! AWESTRUCK GASPS FROM THE AUDIENCE!

A couple of the tricks in this section are true key card tricks. Others take a little liberty with the vocabulary. They use known cards, but not for location purposes. All of the tricks, however, have one thing in common: By identifying just one card, you can work some truly INCREDIBLE magic. And isn't that the KEY point?

SET THE STAGE
No special prep is needed for this trick.

HOT STUFF

This trick is super-simple. You, the magician, must do just two things to make it work:
1. Look at a card without getting caught, and
2. Remember the card for about 30 seconds.
You can handle it, you say? OK, then. Grab an enthusiastic but easily fooled audience member—let's call her Patsy—and give it a whirl.

1 Give Patsy the deck. Ask her to shuffle it as much as she likes, then hand it back to you.

2 Fan the cards facedown. Tell Patsy to pull out any card, look at it, and memorize it.

8

3 Square the deck while Patsy is doing her thing. Split the cards into two piles of any size. Hold one pile in each hand.

4 Is Patsy still memorizing? Good. Casually sneak a peek at either pile's bottom card. Let's say it's the 9♦ Here comes the hardest part of the trick: REMEMBER IT. The 9♦ is your key card.

5 When Patsy is done, tell her to put her card facedown on the OTHER PILE (the one without the 9♦).

6 Put the pile with the 9♦ on top of Patsy's pile. Square the deck.

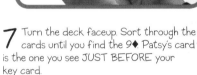

7 Turn the deck faceup. Sort through the cards until you find the 9♦ Patsy's card is the one you see JUST BEFORE your key card.

PATTER PROMPTER

"When you hold a card in your hand, it heats up a little. I happen to have very heat-sensitive fingers, and I can find ANY CARD you have been holding by touch alone."

9

COPYCAT

This trick uses a lot of misdirection. In other words, you do a whole bunch of unnecessary stuff that doesn't affect the trick at all. Your goal is to confuse your viewers and distract them from what you're really doing. The audience member who will be helping you with this trick—let's call him Mark—will be the most bewildered of all.

HIT THE DECK

K♥ is on the bottom of this pile.

3 Pick up the pile that does NOT contain the K♥. DO THIS NO MATTER WHICH PILE MARK TOUCHED. (In magic slang, this move is called a force.) Tell Mark to take the other pile and copy everything you do.

K♥ is on the bottom of this pile.

1 Set the deck facedown on a table. Ask Mark to split it into two piles.

2 Tell Mark to touch either pile.

10

4 Now we're going to confuse the heck out of poor Mark. Take the top card off your pile and slide it into your shoe. Mark does the same.

5 Take the bottom card off your pile and put it into your pocket. Mark does it, too. (If you're paying attention, you know exactly which card that was: the K♥.)

6 Take a card from the middle of your pile and set it facedown on the table. Make sure Mark copies you.

7 By this time, Mark is lost. It's the perfect time to announce that you will identify one of the cards Mark chose. To do so, however, you claim that you must hold Mark's pile. Make the switch. (More misdirection.)

8 Pull any card out of Mark's pile and hold it to your ear. Act like you're listening. Then say, "According to this card, you put the king of hearts in your pocket." Mark, of course, will be skeptical, so he will check to see if you're right. Imagine his LOOK OF SURPRISE when you are!

PATTER PROMPTER

"I've been working with this particular deck of cards for a long time, and I've gotten very friendly with it. In fact, if we do things just right, some of the cards may even TELL ME what's happening to the other cards in the deck."

VISITING CARD

Once you have memorized a couple of cards, this trick is pretty close to foolproof. Just pay attention to the pile that your volunteer—in this case, Patsy—chooses, and you'll be home free.

HIT THE DECK

1 Hand the deck to Patsy, face-down, and tell her to split it roughly in half.

2 Tell Patsy to keep whichever half she likes. Take the rest of the cards.

3 Now let's take a moment to consider the situation. No matter which half Patsy chose, YOU KNOW ONE OF THE CARDS. In other words, Patsy's pile contains either the 3♣ or the 7♦. Let's say Patsy chose the pile with the 3♣. REMEMBER THIS CARD. You can forget about the 7♦. You can actually forget about the position of the 3♣, as well; it doesn't matter.

4 Pull a card from the middle of your pile and look at it. Don't let the audience see it. "It's the three of clubs," you announce. Is it really? NO. You're naming the key card in Patsy's pile. But since the audience can't see your card, they will assume you're telling the truth. (Silly them.) After you make your announcement, place the card facedown on top of your pile.

12

5 Tell Patsy to do the same thing you just did—choose a card, name it out loud, and place it facedown on top of her pile. Let's say she chooses the A♠.

6 You and Patsy both make one complete cut.

7 Hand your pile to Patsy. Ask her to look through the cards and remove the 3♣. Hmmmm...HOW ODD. It isn't there.

8 Ask Patsy to look through her own pile. Patsy will be absolutely astonished when she discovers the 3♣ RIGHT NEXT TO THE A♠ in the middle of the stack!

6

Separate the deck

then move the pile that was originally on top of the deck to the bottom

...AND YOU'RE DONE.

8

PATTER PROMPTER

"Cards are like people in one way: They enjoy hanging out with their friends. Let's see if we can convince two cards of our choice to visit each other. This is going to be tricky, because one of the cards will have to change decks to do it."

13

CLASSROOM CUT-UP

Your buddy Mark chooses a secret card in this trick. Thanks to a sneaky bit of magic, you'll soon figure out which card Mark picks. One hint: Perform this trick AS QUICKLY AS POSSIBLE. It's rather obvious what you're doing, so you must not give your audience time to figure it out.

HIT THE DECK

1 Deal out 16 cards, faceup, in a 4 x 4 grid. Place the cards in the order shown here.

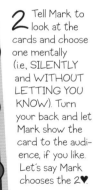

2 Tell Mark to look at the cards and choose one mentally (i.e., SILENTLY and WITHOUT LETTING YOU KNOW). Turn your back and let Mark show the card to the audience, if you like. Let's say Mark chooses the 2♥.

3 When Mark has chosen, ask him which column contains his card. He tells you.

4 Pick up the four cards in Mark's column. Hold them faceup in your hand.

5 Pick up the remaining columns in any order you like. Set them faceup on top of the cards from Mark's column.

6 Turn the cards over. Then deal them out again exactly as you did in Step 1. THIS IS WHERE THE MAGIC HAPPENS. The four cards formerly in Mark's column now form the top row of the card layout.

7 Ask Mark to tell you which column his card is in now. As soon as he does, YOU KNOW HIS CARD. Why? It will always be the top card in the column.

8 Pick up the cards any old way. Hand them to Mark. Let him mix up the pile as much as he wants, then take it back.

9 Start flipping cards faceup onto the table. When you reach the 2♥, announce that you have found what you are looking for. Hold up the card and watch as Mark's mouth falls open in disbelief!

PATTER PROMPTER

"There are 16 card 'students' in my magic class. Most of my students are well behaved, but one naughty card keeps switching seats whenever I turn my back. Let's see if I can figure out which one it is."

15

WHICH ONE?...

This trick starts just like "Classroom Cut-up" on pages 14-15, but the ending is completely different. Instead of simply pulling out Mark's card, you'll reveal it using a method that is guaranteed to BLOW THE MINDS of everyone in your audience.

1 Follow Steps 1 through 6 of "Classroom Cut-up."

2 Pick up the cards any way you like, making ABSOLUTELY SURE that you know the position of Mark's card. For instance, you might pick it up first (very easy to remember) or fourth from last (harder to remember but more deceptive for the audience).

3 Deal the cards facedown in four squares as shown here. Make a mental note of Mark's card.

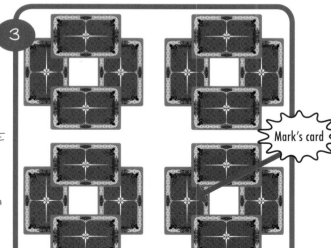

Mark's card

16

4 Now comes the trickery! "Which ones?" you ask Mark, pointing to either the left squares or the right squares. When Mark chooses, you sweep away the squares that DO NOT contain Mark's card. Mark will not question this. After all, you didn't say whether Mark was choosing to keep or get rid of the chosen squares.

5 "Which one?" you ask again, pointing to the two remaining squares. When Mark chooses, remove the square that does not contain Mark's card. IT DOESN'T MATTER IF YOU'RE BEING INCONSISTENT. Just keep going and no one will notice.

6 Now indicate either the top/bottom or right/left edges of the final square. "Which ones?" Let Mark speak, then remove the appropriate cards.

7 Now you are left with just two cards on the table. "Which one?" you ask for the last time. Mark chooses; you remove.

8 Tell Mark to flip over the sole remaining card. It's the one you forced, of course. You had it pegged from the very beginning. But to the audience, it will appear that Mark did all the choosing. So everyone will be DUMBFOUNDED when the correct card appears!

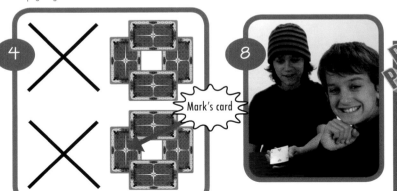

Mark's card

Mark's card

PATTER PROMPTER

"Some people have a natural bond with cards. I can sense that you, sir, are one of them. In fact, your bond is so strong that I think the cards might just arrange themselves according to your will. Would you care to help me with a little demonstration?"

17

SECTION

2: MIND-READING CARD TRICKS

Did you know that some of the best magicians aren't really magicians at all? They are actually PSYCHICS who can identify cards through MENTAL TELEPATHY ALONE! Their brains are MUTANT ORGANS where electrical impulses zip around at SEVENTEEN TIMES the rate of a normal human being!

Ummm, OK. Patsy and Mark might buy that one, but not YOU. You're much too savvy. So let's get real here.

The truth is, magicians are not psychics or mind-readers, and they can't really use their brains to control or identify cards. But they DO know some tricks that make it LOOK that way. And in magic, people tend to believe what they see—or "think" they see, anyway.

SET THE STAGE

Before the show, remove any card from the deck. For this example, let's say your card is the 8♠. Write "eight of spades" on a piece of paper. Put the paper into an envelope, then seal the envelope. Place the envelope and the card in your pocket.

THE ENVELOPE, PLEASE

In this trick, Mark isn't working with a full deck. And he doesn't have all the cards he should have, either. HAR-DEE-HAR-HAR! Just a little magician humor for you.

HIT THE DECK

1 Hand Mark the deck with the missing card. Ask him to shuffle the deck as much as he likes, then set it facedown on a table.

2 Pull out the prepared envelope. "This envelope contains my prediction," you announce grandly. BEHIND the envelope, out of sight of the audience, you hold the card you removed from the deck.

3 Set the envelope and the hidden card on top of the deck.

4 Ask Mark to pick up the envelope, open it, and read your prediction.

5 Now ask Mark to flip over the top card. There in Mark's hand is the 8♠—the EXACT CARD YOU PREDICTED! Ooooh, ahhh!

PATTER PROMPTER

"As I was preparing for this show, I had a very strong vision of a certain card. The vision was so intense that I wrote down the name of the card I saw. I have a feeling that the card might just appear during this trick!"

19

SET THE STAGE
Make two copies of the list on this page. Keep one. Give the other to a friend who will not be at your magic show.
Tell the friend to expect a phone call at a certain time.

PHONE A FRIEND

Do you believe in ESP? Actually, it doesn't really matter what you believe. After seeing this trick in action, your AUDIENCE will be believers, and that's the important thing. All you need is a volunteer. (And a photocopier, and a phone, and a friend to play psychic.)

Value:
Ace   Carey (Carrie)
2   Chris
3   Francis (Frances)
4   Jamie
5   Gene (Jean)
6   Jesse (Jessie)
7   Lee
8   Nicky
9   Pat
10   Ray (Rae)
Jack   Ryan
Queen Shawn
King   Terry

Suit:
Clubs   Collins
Diamonds   Daniels
Hearts   Hughes
Spades   Smith

20

HIT THE DECK

1 Tell Patsy to pick any card from a full deck. In this example, let's say she chooses the Q♦. Patsy shows the card to everyone, including you.

3 Hand Patsy a phone. Tell her to dial your waiting friend's number and ask for Shawn Daniels (or whatever name matches the actual card chosen).

4 When your friend hears Patsy's request, he or she checks the list and sees that "Shawn Daniels" stands for the Q♦ The friend proceeds to "read" Patsy's mind and name her card, much to the astonishment of everyone!

Queen   Shawn

Diamonds   Daniels

2 Pull out the list you copied. Find the first name that goes with queen and the last name that goes with diamonds. To mask what you're doing, tell the audience that the paper shows the phone number of your psychic pal. Or if you want to get REALLY FANCY, you can memorize the list.

PATTER PROMPTER

"I have the name and phone number of an actual psychic in my pocket. This psychic is going to read someone's mind RIGHT OVER THE PHONE. Who wants to volunteer?"

TATTLETALE QUEEN...

HIT THE DECK

Didn't your mother ever tell you that no one likes a tattletale? Well, this trick proves that Mom isn't always right. EVERYONE will like this tale-telling queen—even Mark, your victim for this particular magic-go-round.

1 Hand Mark the deck, facedown. Let him shuffle the deck as much as he likes, then you take it back.

2 Turn the deck faceup and start thumbing through it. As you do, memorize the first two cards. Let's say they are the 4♦ and the 10♣. BE QUICK! You don't want anyone to know you were paying special attention to these cards.

22

3 Keep sorting through the deck until you find the Q♠ (see Patter Prompter). Pull it out and show it to the audience.

4 Hand the rest of the cards, facedown, to Mark. Tell him to cut the deck wherever he likes.

5 After Mark cuts, you take the top pile. Do anything you want with it; it's not important. Let Mark keep the bottom pile. Tell him to deal it facedown into two stacks, alternating between left and right each time he puts down a card.

6 When Mark is done, hold the Q♠ up to your ear. Pretend you are listening hard.

7 After you have listened long enough, tell the audience that the queen has identified the two cards on top of Mark's piles. Name the cards you memorized earlier. Mark turns them over and sure enough, you're right!

PATTER PROMPTER

"Did you know that the queen of spades has special mental powers? It's true! Let me just look through the deck and pull her out. She's going to help me identify two cards in this astonishing trick."

23

SET THE STAGE

Arrange the deck so all the black cards are on top and all the red cards are on the bottom. HINT: The order of the cards is not actually important. It's just a clever bit of misdirection that will help you gather the information you need.

PSYCHIC SANDWICH

Sometimes "forgetting a step"—on purpose, of course—is a useful tool. It lets you go back and redo parts of a trick in a slightly different way, thus creating some truly MIRACULOUS results.

HIT THE DECK

1 Tell our old friend Patsy that the black and red cards are all bunched together from a previous trick. Show her, if you like. Hand the deck to Patsy and ask her to shuffle well.

2 When Patsy is satisfied, take the deck back. Turn it faceup and thumb through the cards very quickly, as if you're making sure they are well mixed. THIS IS NOT WHAT YOU'RE REALLY DOING. Your true goal is to see and memorize the top and bottom cards in the deck. Let's say the top and bottom cards are the A♥ and the 8♠.

3 Write "ace of hearts" and "eight of spades" on a piece of paper. Fold it in half.

4 Square the deck and hold it facedown. Ask Patsy to stick the paper into the middle of the deck.

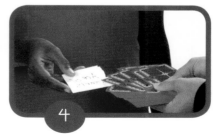

24

5 After Patsy does this, slap yourself in the forehead and cry, "RATS! I forgot a step." Cut the deck where the paper is inserted and let the paper fall to the floor, as if by accident. You are now holding part of the deck in each hand. Tell Patsy, "I want you to pick up that paper and LOOK AT WHAT I WROTE. That way, you will know I haven't switched the paper in some way."

6 When Patsy is done with her task, hold out the pile that was ON TOP before. Tell Patsy to set the paper on the pile.

7 Put the other pile on top and square the deck. Did you see what just happened? Your paper is now sandwiched between the A♥ and the 8♠—YES, the very ones you memorized.

8 Hand the deck to Patsy. Tell her to check the cards on either side of your paper. You got it—they are the ones you predicted. Patsy shows the paper to everyone to prove it's true!

PATTER PROMPTER

"I'm feeling especially psychic today. I have a hunch that by using my mental powers, I can identify not just ONE card but TWO. Let's give it a try!"

25

MENTAL BOND

This trick is SO STUPENDOUS, SO ASTRONOMICAL, that no single deck of cards can possibly HARNESS ITS POWER. Yes, you actually need TWO FULL REGULAR DECKS OF CARDS to perform this one. OK, it's a pain to find the extra cards, but it's well worth it. Mark and the rest of your audience members will thank you for your effort.

HIT THE DECK

1 Hand one deck to Mark. You keep the other one.

2 Both of you shuffle well. When you're done shuffling, sneak a quick peek at the deck's bottom card. Let's say it's the 5♣. REMEMBER THIS CARD.

3 Switch decks with Mark. Instruct him to take a card from the middle of the deck, memorize it, and then put it facedown on top of the deck. You do the same thing— or at least, that's what it looks like. Actually, you only PRETEND to memorize your card. You don't really have to do it.

4 Tell Mark to cut his deck several times. You do it too. Then switch decks again.

26

5 Say, "Now I have your deck and you have my deck, right? I'm going to look through the deck I'm holding and remove the SAME CARD I put on top of the other deck." (Misdirection here; all this blather doesn't mean a thing. But everyone will THINK it does.) Look through the deck and find the 5♣, the card you really memorized. The card Mark chose—in this case, the J♦—is just beneath your card.

6 Pull out the J♦ and set it facedown on the table.

7 Tell Mark to look through his deck and remove the card he chose. At this point you know which card Mark is removing, right? YEP, it's the J♦ He places this card facedown on the table next to yours.

8 At the same time, both of you flip your cards over. Everyone but YOU will be astonished to see that they match!

Mark's card

Your card

"Let's try very hard to reach out to each other with our minds...OK, it's working, I can feel you. We have a bond now and I think it's strong enough to help us pick the VERY SAME CARD from two different decks."

SECTION

3: MARKED CARD TRICKS

One of the easiest ways to identify a card is to mark it in some way. A good mark is subtle, so it will not be noticed by the audience or any helpers you use. But it is blindingly obvious to YOU, THE MAGICIAN. (DUH—you know what you're looking for. That tends to make things a little easier.) Using the mark, you can instantly zoom in on the card you need and create your magical effect. TAH-DAH!

911 NOTE: In tricks that require volunteers to choose cards, your marked card may be selected by sheer chance. If this happens, DON'T PANIC. Your trick is not ruined. You may have to adjust your patter a little bit, but that's OK; a good magician is always ready to improvise.

SET THE STAGE

Push hard with a pencil point to make little round dents in all four corners of the A♦. Erase the marks. Make sure you can easily feel the dents.

HUMAN SCALE

Human fingers are incredibly sensitive. Blind people can actually read with their fingertips by brushing them over raised dent patterns. In this trick, you will take advantage of this fact to fool poor Patsy YET AGAIN.

28

HIT THE DECK

1 Ask Patsy to blindfold you.

2 Hand Patsy the deck with the dented ace. Tell her to shuffle the deck as much as she likes, then return it to you.

3 Sort through the deck, touching each card's corner as you go. Every now and then you can pretend to "weigh" a card in your hand. When you find the A♦, pull it out and hold it up. You're still blindfolded, but you're holding the CORRECT CARD!

4 Repeat Steps 2 and 3 several times if you wish to amaze your audience even more.

PATTER PROMPTER

"With practice, it is possible to tell cards apart by their weight! To prove it, I will identify the ace of diamonds by FEEL ALONE. This card is unique because it has the least ink of any card in the deck. That makes it the LIGHTEST card."

SALTY SURPRISE

Your friend Mark is about to get a little SALT in his magical diet. The result is one truly tasty trick!

HIT THE DECK

1 Set a deck of cards facedown on a table. Tell Mark to pick up about half the deck, leaving the rest of the pile on the table, and look at the bottom card. Let's say it's the 6♥.

2 While Mark does this, put your hand into your pocket. Press a fingertip firmly against the salt. A few grains will stick to your skin.

3 Pull your hand out of your pocket. Use your salty fingertip to touch the pile on the table. SECRET MAGICAL STUFF: When you do this, you will leave a little bit of SALT on the top card to mark your place. "Put your pile back down," you say to Mark.

4 After Mark replaces his pile, you square the deck. Then smack the edge of the deck with your palm. The cards will fan out, leaving one especially large break.

5 Pick up the cards above the large break. ALAKAZAM! It's the 6♥!

Smack along this edge

Largest break

PATTER PROMPTER

"Sometimes it's possible to startle cards into doing what you want them to do. I'm going to hit the deck rather sharply. At the same time, I want everyone to shout along with me, 'OUT!!!' Maybe we can surprise the right card into appearing."

RISING TO THE TOP

Our friend Patsy has been fooled so many times, she's probably feeling a little overwhelmed by now. In this trick, you will make her feel a little better by "giving" her some incredible mental powers.

HIT THE DECK

1 Fan the deck. Hold the cards out facedown and let Patsy choose any one she likes. Tell Patsy to look at the card and remember it. Let's say she chooses the 10♠.

2 Tell Patsy to replace the card wherever she likes. HERE'S THE TRICK: Make sure you're holding the cards very tightly so Patsy cannot push her card all the way in. You finish pushing it in yourself with a fingernail. This will leave a small dent in the card's edge.

3 Hand the deck to Patsy and let her rearrange it as much as she wants to.

4 When Patsy is satisfied, take the deck and look at its edge. You will instantly see the card you marked. Tell Patsy to concentrate (see the Patter Prompter section), then cut the deck right above the marked card.

PATTER PROMPTER

"Patsy, I want you to concentrate VERY HARD on the card you chose. Think about it RISING, RISING, RISING. By doing this, you will force your card to the top of the pile."

31

BEST FRIENDS...

To pull off this trick, you really have to watch the deck and keep track of its position. In a way, it's NOT FAIR. You're doing all this hidden dirty work—VERY SKILLFULLY, we might add. But no one sees it. Meanwhile, Patsy and Mark appear to have amazing magical abilities. Oh, well. Sometimes you gotta take one for the team.

Marked card

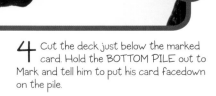

4

HIT THE DECK

1 Fan the deck facedown in such a way that your dots do not show. (Test this for yourself first. The dots ALWAYS show when you fan the deck in one direction, NEVER in the other direction.)

2 Tell Mark to remove any card and memorize it. Let's say Mark chooses the 7♣.

3 While Mark is doing this, square the deck and reverse it. In other words, turn it so the edge that formerly faced Mark now faces you and vice-versa. Thumb through the cards until you see your mark. (The dot will be easy to see now that the deck is reversed.)

4 Cut the deck just below the marked card. Hold the BOTTOM PILE out to Mark and tell him to put his card facedown on the pile.

5 Put the piles back together. POP QUIZ: Where is your marked card? Yep, that's right—it's on top of the 7♣. You get an A+.

6 Square the deck, then hand it to Mark. Tell him to CUT (NOT SHUFFLE) the cards as many times as he likes, then return the deck to you.

7 Now it's time for Round Two. With Patsy's help, repeat Steps 1 through 6. Let's say Patsy chooses the 3♦. At the end of this process, here's what the situation looks like:

8 Tell Patsy and Mark to hold hands and concentrate on the cards they picked. (Check out the Patter Prompter for the reasoning behind this step.)

9 Cut the deck right under the marked card. Ask Patsy to remove the card at the cut and look at it. HOCUS-POCUS! It's the 3♦!

10 Now ask Mark to remove the next card. SHAZAAM! Yep, it's the 7♣!

11. IN CASE OF EMERGENCY:
If your marked card ends up as the bottom card or the second card from the bottom, you must alter the end of the trick.

If the marked card is on the bottom: You know Patsy's card is on top of the deck and Mark's card is just below. No cutting is required.

If the marked card is second from the bottom: You know Patsy's card is on the bottom of the deck and Mark's card is on top. Tell your volunteers to remove the appropriate cards. Then sit back and wait for the CRIES OF DELIGHT!

4

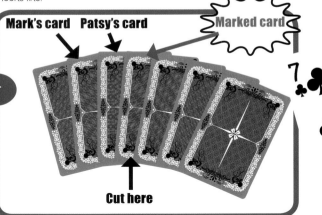

Mark's card **Patsy's card** **Marked card**

Cut here

PATTER PROMPTER

"I need two volunteers who are willing to get a little CLOSE to each other. By doing this, you're going to make two cards of your choice come together in the deck. You might say they're going to be best friends!"

SECTION

4: ARRANGED DECKS

You can create a lot of INCREDIBLE ILLUSIONS by arranging decks ahead of time. There's just one problem with arranged decks: You can't let audience members examine the cards closely, or even handle them AT ALL in some cases. This naturally makes people suspicious. So in any magic show, it's best to use arranged decks sparingly.

Here's another tip: Do any tricks that require a certain card order FIRST. After you have flawlessly performed the trick and enjoyed the audience's applause, shuffle the deck several times. In the magic biz (as in the crime biz), this is known as "GETTING RID OF THE EVIDENCE."

PAMPERED PAIR

Most people are pretty trusting. They want to believe what you tell them. A good magician UNDERSTANDS this trait, SALUTES it, and then EXPLOITS it for his or her personal benefit.

3 Pull off the top two cards—the K♠ and the Q♣—and show them to the audience. They're totally different cards, of course. But if you move quickly, the audience will THINK they are the same pair, and that's all that matters.

1 Pull the top two cards—the K♣ and the Q♠—off the deck. Flash them briefly at the audience, then stick them into the middle of the pile.

2 Tap the top of the pile and say a magical word of your choice.

PATTER PROMPTER

"This king and queen are a little full of themselves. They always think they deserve to be above the other cards. If you stick them somewhere else–in the middle of the deck, for instance–they just pop right back to the top!"

35

ROLL OVER, ROVER

This is one of the simplest tricks in the book, and one of the most effective. It uses some very basic sleight of hand. In other words, you have to change some things about the deck without the audience noticing. Don't worry; it's not too tough. They have no idea what to look for, so unless you do something really BONE-HEADED, you should be home free.

1 Fan the deck, facedown, and hold it out toward our faithful buddy Patsy. MAKE SURE NO ONE SEES YOUR SINGLE FACEUP CARD. Tell Patsy to choose any card from the middle of the deck, look at it, and memorize it. Let's say her card is the 4♥.

2 While Patsy is busy, casually flip the deck over. The deck LOOKS just the same—but in reality, every card except the top one is now FACEUP.

3 Tell Patsy to stick her card, facedown, anywhere in the pile. After she does this, casually flip the deck over again. Babbling about something meaningless is a good way to distract the audience during this move.

4 Look through the deck. You'll know Patsy's card as soon as you see it, of course, because it's the only faceup card! (Actually, that's not quite true. The bottom one is still faceup, but you won't let the audience see THAT one.)

PATTER PROMPTER

"You can train cards just like dogs. I've been working with this particular deck, and our training is coming along nicely. When I shout 'Roll over, Rover,' the card you chose will actually FLIP OVER in the deck!"

36

LET ME OUT!

You have to be verrrry careful not to get caught on this one. The pre-arrangement of the deck is pretty dramatic, so the audience MUST NOT see the cards while you work. And if you plan to use the deck again, you need to SHUFFLE and SHUFFLE and SHUFFLE AGAIN when the trick is over.

HIT THE DECK

3

1 Tell Mark to choose a card from the middle of the deck and memorize it. (PSST: It will ALWAYS be a red card.) Let's say Mark chooses the 5♥.

2 Have Mark place his card facedown on top of the deck. Hand him the deck and let him CUT (NOT SHUFFLE) as often as he likes, then return the deck to you.

3 Thumb through the cards WITHOUT LETTING THE AUDIENCE SEE THEIR FACES. (They might find the color arrangement suspicious, don't you think?) When you spot a red card between two black cards, you'll know you have found Mark's little secret. Reveal the card to your stunned audience!

PATTER PROMPTER

"Once you take a card out of the deck, it doesn't want to go back in. If you know how to listen, you can hear it SHOUTING and SHOUTING to be taken out again. All this racket will lead me straight to the card Mark just chose."

37

SEVEN UP

There's nothing terribly clever about this trick. Once the cards have been arranged, the sneaky stuff takes care of itself. All you have to do is spell a few words correctly. Just remember: TWO and FOUR are numbers. TO and FOR are prepositions. NOW IS NOT THE TIME TO GET CONFUSED ABOUT THESE THINGS!

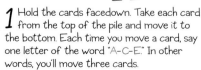

HIT THE DECK

1 Hold the cards facedown. Take each card from the top of the pile and move it to the bottom. Each time you move a card, say one letter of the word "A-C-E." In other words, you'll move three cards.

2 When you are done spelling ACE, flip up the next card and set it on the table. HEY! It's the ACE! How could you possibly know that?

3 Repeat Steps 1 and 2 with the remaining cards. But this time, spell the word "T-W-O." The card you flip up will indeed be the 2. YOU DID IT!

5 Now spell "F-O-U-R," then "F-I-V-E," then "S-I-X." Each time you finish spelling a word, flip a card onto the table. You're RIGHT, RIGHT, RIGHT.

6 When just one card remains, hold it up dramatically with its back to the audience. Announce, "We've already found every card from ace through six. So this one must be the..." (fling it down) "...SEVEN!" You're correct, of course!

4 Do it again, this time spelling the word "T-H-R-E-E." Care to take a wild guess which card appears at the end?

PATTER PROMPTER

"I've gathered cards showing ace through 7 in this pile. Right now the cards are all mixed up. (Flash the cards at the audience if you like so they can see it's true.) But if we call their names, maybe we can convince them to line up in order."

KINGS' DAY OUT

This entire trick is **ONE BIG MISDIRECTION.** Everything you tell your volunteer to do is unnecessary; you could get the same effect by flipping over the top four cards right off the bat. But what fun would THAT be? It's much more interesting for both you AND the audience to add a bunch of "mysterious" cutting and dealing.

HIT THE DECK

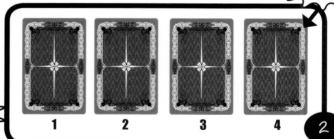

Kings are here.

Kings are here.

1 Hand the deck facedown to Patsy. Ask her to split it roughly in half and set both halves right next to each other on a table. REMEMBER WHICH PILE HAS THE KINGS.

2 Now ask Patsy to split each pile in half again. Tell her to put the new piles right next to the old piles so the cards form a row. After Patsy does this, the pile with the kings will be AT ONE END OF THE ROW. In this picture, let's assume the kings are in **Pile 4**.

Kings are here.

Patsy picks up this pile.

3 Tell Patsy to pick up the pile at the OTHER END of the row—in this example, **Pile 1**. Have her deal three cards onto the spot where **Pile 1** used to be. Then have her deal one card onto each of the other three piles. When Patsy finishes this task, tell her to put **Pile 1** back in its original position.

4 Next, tell Patsy to pick up **Pile 2**. Patsy deals three cards onto the spot where **Pile 2** used to be, then one card onto the other three piles. She sets **Pile 2** down in its original place.

Deal one card onto each of the other three piles.

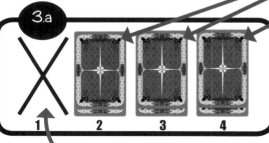

Then put Pile 1 back in its original position.

5 Patsy repeats the process with **Pile 3**.

6 Now we come to the key pile! Patsy goes through the whole process again. THIS IS WHERE THE MAGIC HAPPENS. Because of the way you arranged the cards earlier, the four kings end up on top of the four piles.

7 Look at your watch and say, "It's time! The kings must be ready by now." Tell Patsy to flip up the top card on each pile. The audience will be FLABBERGASTED when the kings appear one by one!

PATTER PROMPTER

"The four kings were talking last night, and they decided to get together today and play golf. They agreed to meet each other (check your watch) right about now. Patsy, why don't you come up here and help me for a minute? Let's see if we can pull this foursome out of the deck—without ever looking at the cards."

41

SECTION

5: SELF-WORKING CARD TRICKS

Self-working card tricks are all about math. There is no need for you to BORE YOURSELF with the exact principles at work. You don't have to understand them. You DO, however, have to be able to do some number juggling. In some cases, you must even do these things IN YOUR HEAD. Practice these tricks well before you perform them to prevent yourself from goofing up.

Once you've got the hang of it, you'll be VERY HAPPY you made the effort. The great thing about self-working card tricks is that they create truly PERPLEXING results with absolutely no magical mischief on your part. So no matter how smart or observant your audience is, they will NEVER figure out how you pulled these tricks off!

DIZZY DECK

Let's start with a very, very easy one. Assuming you can manage a simple deck flip without being caught, math makes it nearly IMPOSSIBLE for this trick to fail.

HIT THE DECK

1 Deal 26 cards (half the deck) faceup into a pile. Set the rest of the deck facedown on the same pile.

2 Hand the deck to your old pal Mark. Tell him to shuffle it thoroughly, so the faceup and facedown cards are all mixed up.

3 When Mark is done, have him deal the cards into two equal piles. Tell him to hand you either pile and keep the other one for himself.

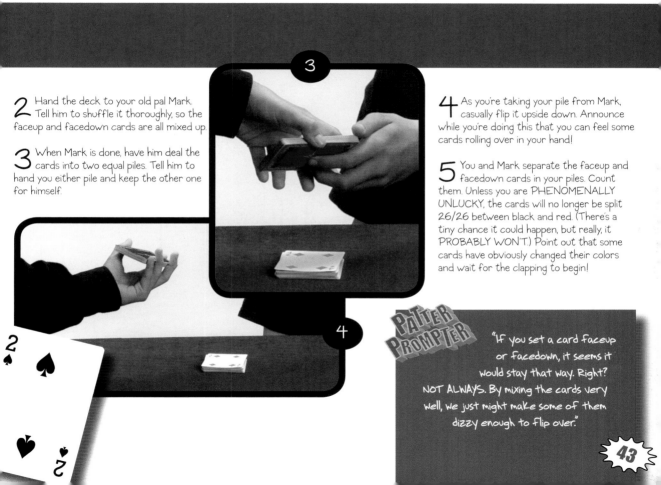

4 As you're taking your pile from Mark, casually flip it upside down. Announce while you're doing this that you can feel some cards rolling over in your hand!

5 You and Mark separate the faceup and facedown cards in your piles. Count them. Unless you are PHENOMENALLY UNLUCKY, the cards will no longer be split 26/26 between black and red. (There's a tiny chance it could happen, but really, it PROBABLY WON'T.) Point out that some cards have obviously changed their colors and wait for the clapping to begin!

PATTER PROMPTER

"If you set a card faceup or facedown, it seems it would stay that way. Right? NOT ALWAYS. By mixing the cards very well, we just might make some of them dizzy enough to flip over."

43

TWENTY-ONE

Some magicians do Step 4 of this trick behind their backs or beneath a handkerchief. They do this because a really math-savvy volunteer might figure out the trick after seeing how the cards are dealt. Is Patsy that smart? NAAAAH. Ninety-nine percent of the time (there's some MATH for you!), you can get away with doing this trick right under her gullible nose.

HIT THE DECK

1 Tell Patsy to think of a number between 1 and 10. For this example, let's say she thinks of 7. Let Patsy shuffle the deck as much as she likes. (Misdirection. Not important.)

2 Instruct Patsy to hold the deck facedown. Then tell her to deal cards faceup onto the table, one by one. She speaks a number as she deals each card: "ONE-TWO-THREE..." etc. When Patsy reaches "SEVEN," she stops dealing. She memorizes the card she just laid down—in this example, the J♥.

44

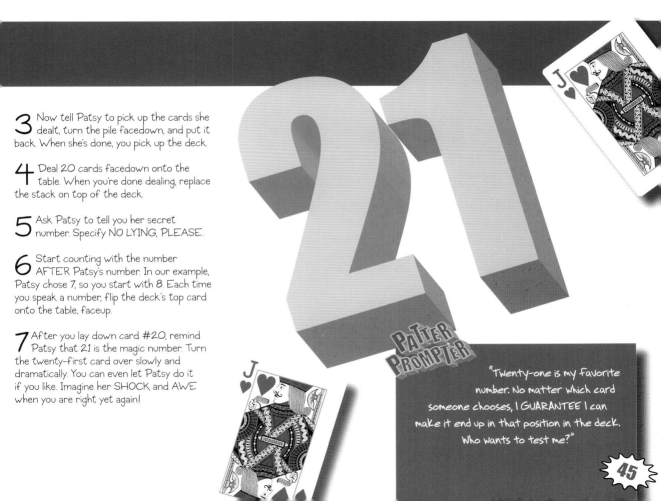

3 Now tell Patsy to pick up the cards she dealt, turn the pile facedown, and put it back. When she's done, you pick up the deck.

4 Deal 20 cards facedown onto the table. When you're done dealing, replace the stack on top of the deck.

5 Ask Patsy to tell you her secret number. Specify NO LYING, PLEASE.

6 Start counting with the number AFTER Patsy's number. In our example, Patsy chose 7, so you start with 8. Each time you speak a number, flip the deck's top card onto the table, faceup.

7 After you lay down card #20, remind Patsy that 21 is the magic number. Turn the twenty-first card over slowly and dramatically. You can even let Patsy do it if you like. Imagine her SHOCK and AWE when you are right yet again!

PATTER PROMPTER

"Twenty-one is my favorite number. No matter which card someone chooses, I GUARANTEE I can make it end up in that position in the deck. Who wants to test me?"

THIRTEEN...

This trick is LONG but SPECTACULAR. It's a little heavy on the counting and adding. But if you take the time to figure it out, you'll be happy you did. The effect here is so BAFFLING and yet so FOOLPROOF, it's a great addition to any magic act.

HIT THE DECK

1 Hand the deck facedown to Mark. Let him shuffle as much as he likes.

2 Now tell Mark to flip the top card, faceup, onto the table. Note the card's number value. In this trick, jacks have a value of 11, queens have a value of 12, and kings have a value of 13.

3 Mark flips another card faceup onto the pile, counting out loud as he does. He starts with the number AFTER the value of the first card. So if the first card is a 3, for instance, Mark will start with 4. Mark counts out loud, "FOUR-FIVE-SIX," etc., until he reaches 13. He flips down a card each time he speaks a number.

5

4 When you're sure Mark knows what he's doing, turn your back so no one can accuse you of looking.

5 Mark keeps making piles using this method, with one difference. Now that he has the hang of things, tell him to count SILENTLY so you, the magician, will not know the bottom cards on each pile. He does this over and over until he doesn't have enough cards to complete the last pile (i.e., to count all the way to 13). He places these cards aside.

6 Now tell Mark to choose any three piles and turn them facedown. The other piles plus the incomplete pile are gathered into one big stack and given to you.

7 Tell Mark to turn over the top cards on any two of the piles.

8 OK, you can turn around now. Look at the two faceup cards and mentally add their values. In this example, $6 + 8 = 14$.

$6+8=14$

PATTER PROMPTER

"Some people think the number 13 is unlucky. Not me! For me, 13 has always been a LUCKY number. Let's work the number 13 into this trick and see if it will make me lucky enough to guess a mystery card."

47

9 Mentally add 10 to the total. 14 + 10 = 24.

14+10=24

10 Deal off the appropriate number of cards (in this case, 24) from the pile you're holding.

11 Without a pause, count the remaining cards (mentally again, of course). As an example, let's assume that 11 cards remain. This number is ALWAYS the value of the card on top of the last pile.

12

12 Announce the value of the card—in this case, a jack. Lift it and hold it up so everyone can see. THERE IS NO WAY YOU COULD HAVE KNOWN THAT—YET YOU DID. It's MATH AT WORK, thank you very much!

SET THE STAGE

Practice A LOT. There are tons of steps here—and since you won't be watching your helper, you need to give VERY CLEAR instructions.

MONEY TALKS...

It seems like you don't have much to do in this trick. After all, your back is turned until Step 11. But as always, you have the MOST IMPORTANT JOB OF ALL. You have to really understand what you're doing, and you have to communicate it to a smart volunteer. Hmmm, Patsy might not quite fit THAT particular bill. But let's ask her to help anyway and hope for the best.

HIT THE DECK

1 Set a deck of cards, a piece of paper, and a pencil on a table. Then turn your back to the audience and take a few steps away from the table. This makes it clear that you're not participating in ANY WAY.

2 Tell Patsy to take any coin from her pocket. (She can borrow one from another audience member if she doesn't have one.)

3 Ask Patsy if her coin was issued in 1991 or 2002. If she says "Yes," tell her to choose another coin. Give her any excuse you like. If she says "No," go on with the trick.

4 Tell Patsy to write down the coin's year of issue WITHOUT TELLING YOU. For this example, let's say the date on the coin is 1998.

PATTER PROMPTER

"There's an old saying: Money talks. You're about to see how true this saying really is. In this trick, a volunteer's money will magically tell me the identity of a secret card!"

49

4

5 Now tell Patsy to REVERSE the year and write that number down, too. 1998 reversed is 8991.

6 Tell Patsy to subtract the smaller number from the larger number. 8991 – 1998 = 6993.

7 Tell Patsy to remove cards matching this number from the deck. In this example, Patsy would remove a 6, two 9s, and a 3. If Patsy's number includes any zeros, she should pull out jacks instead. THERE IS ONE RULE: The four cards must include one of each suit. In other words, there will be just one club, one diamond, one heart, and one spade.

8 At this point you may want to ask the audience to check up on Patsy. DO NOT GO ON until several people agree that Patsy has correctly followed your instructions!

9 When you're fairly sure that Patsy is not messing up your trick, tell her to turn her four cards facedown. Ask her to rearrange the cards until she no longer knows which is which.

8991-1998=6993

7

10 Tell Patsy to choose any one of the cards and place it, WITHOUT LOOKING AT IT, in her pocket

11 FINALLY, you get to turn around. Take the remaining three cards from Patsy and look at them. First notice what suit is missing—in our example, a ♣ This is the suit of the card Patsy chose.

12 Now add the values of the three cards. In our example, the remaining cards add up to $9 + 9 + 3 = 21$.

$$9 + 9 + 3 = 21$$

10

MULTIPLES OF 9:
9, 18, 27, 36

13 SUBTRACT this number from the next highest multiple of 9. (This sounds harder than it is. There are only four numbers to remember; check out the box in the upper righthand corner of this page.) The answer is the value of the missing card. In our example, $27 - 21 = 6$.

$$27 - 21 = 6$$

14 You now know the value and suit (6♣) of the card in Patsy's pocket. Reveal this information, then have Patsy pull out her card and show it to everyone. GASP! IT CAN'T BE TRUE!!

Magicians have a racy word for the type of trick deck that comes with this book. It's almost embarrassing to say it, but if you're going to be a REAL MAGICIAN, you must know the lingo...so here goes. It's called a STRIPPER DECK. It gets this name from the fact that one edge is partly STRIPPED OFF, or TAPERED. This makes the deck slightly narrower along one edge than the other. The taper is so subtle that your audience will never spot it, even if you let them handle the cards. But because YOU know what to look for, you can use your tapered deck to do some truly AWE-INSPIRING things.

SET THE STAGE

Make sure all the cards in the deck are tapered in the same direction. (All of the edges should feel perfectly smooth when the deck is squared.)

SWIRLING AURA

The key move in all "stripper deck" tricks is the deck reverse. You already learned this technique in "Best Friends" on pages 32-33. But you're going to be using it a lot more over the next few pages. So let's do a VERY BASIC TRICK that will help you get REALLY GOOD at this switch.

HIT THE DECK

1 Fan the cards and hold them out, face-down, toward Mark. Tell him to choose any card, look at it, and memorize it.

2 While Mark is doing this, square the deck and very casually turn it around. The edge that was formerly facing you is now facing Mark. More important, THE TAPER HAS BEEN REVERSED.

3 Tell Mark to stick his card back into the deck anywhere he likes.

4 Cut the deck several times. Square it and look at the edges. You will immediately see one corner of Mark's card sticking out a little beyond the others. Pull out the card and show it to your stunned audience!

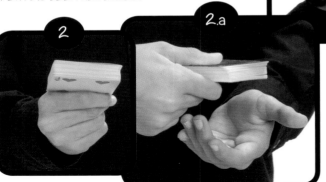

PATTER PROMPTER

"Every person has an aura. It's like a colorful cloud around the body. Most people can't see auras–but I CAN. I can even tell which card someone touches, because a little bit of their aura clings to the card."

53

PICKPOCKET

You might want to pick a same-sex volunteer for this trick. WHY? Because you're going to stick your hand right into your volunteer's pants pocket. It's a little awkward—but the effect is SO worth it.

1 You already know the basic move, so let's condense it all into one step. Tell Mark to choose a card and memorize it. Secretly reverse the deck. Tell Mark to replace the card.

2 Hand the deck to Mark and let him CUT it as many times as he likes. When he's done, tell him to put the entire deck into his pocket.

3 Reach into Mark's pocket and touch the long edges of the deck. It will be easy to feel one card sticking out past the others. Put one finger on either side of the deck and squeeze, trapping the reversed card.

4 Quickly pull your hand—and the card—from Mark's pocket. Mark WON'T BELIEVE HIS EYES when he sees what you are holding!

4

PATTER PROMPTER

"Before I was a magician, I spent some time on the streets. I won't tell you what I did there. Let's just say that some of my street skills come in VERY HANDY in my magic act."

54

SLIPPERY JACK

This trick uses a clever bit of magic called the double lift. It looks like you're picking up one card—but you're actually holding TWO CARDS. The double lift is extra simple when you're using a stripper deck, as you'll see when you practice this great trick.

HIT THE DECK

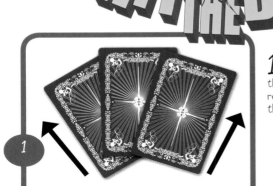

1 Hold the deck facedown with the wide ends of the reversed cards facing the audience.

PATTER PROMPTER

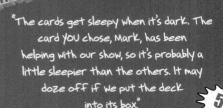

"The cards get sleepy when it's dark. The card you chose, Mark, has been helping with our show, so it's probably a little sleepier than the others. It may doze off if we put the deck into its box."

55

2 Squeeze the reversed cards' wide edges and lift the top two cards at once. To the audience, it looks like you're only holding one card. What they actually see, of course, is the SECOND card from the top (the jack of diamonds); the true top card is hidden.

3 Put the cards back on the deck.

4 Now remove the REAL top card. Lay it face down on a table WITHOUT SHOWING IT TO THE AUDIENCE. Everyone will assume this is the card they just saw.

5 Time to call upon our much-abused helper, Patsy. Tell her, "Put your finger on the jack, please. I want to make sure he CANNOT escape!" Patsy does as you ask.

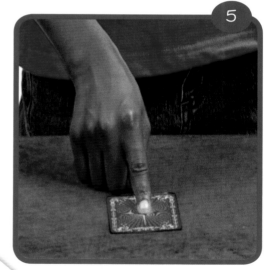

6 Cut the deck several times. Keep asking Patsy if the jack is still trapped. Patsy will keep telling you that he is.

7 When the deck is well mixed, tell Patsy to lift her finger and look at the trapped card. Shake your head disgustedly when you see that it is the WRONG CARD. "You let the jack escape! Now I have to find him," you say. Meanwhile, the audience sits in STUNNED SILENCE, amazed that the jack somehow SLIPPED AWAY without Patsy's knowledge.

8 Feel the edges of the deck. You will immediately find the only reversed card. It's the jack, of course. Now you can cut to it, pull it right out, or reveal it in any other way you like.

PATTER PROMPTER

"The jack of diamonds is a slippery guy. You have to watch him EVERY SECOND or he'll run away."

SET THE STAGE

Using the tapered deck of cards, reverse the ace of spades. Replace it anywhere in the deck.

ALWAYS ACE

Poor Patsy and Mark. You have fooled them OVER and OVER and OVER, and their self-esteem must be taking a real beating. For the book's GRAND FINALE, why don't you pick on some OTHER audience members for a change?

1 Hand the deck to any audience member. Tell him or her to CUT the deck as much as desired, then hand it back to you.

2 Cut the deck seemingly at random. What you're REALLY doing, however, is feeling for your reversed card, then cutting just below that card.

3 Lift the top pile and let the audience member look at the bottom card. It's the ace, of course. But you don't even look at the card, so to your helper, there doesn't seem to be ANY WAY you could know that. Tell your unsuspecting target to remember the card.

4 Put the deck back together and hand it to another audience member. Go through the same process. Once again you cut STRAIGHT TO THE ACE. Tell your current helper to remember the card.

5 Repeat the whole thing with as many audience members as you like.

6 When you feel you have roped in enough victims, set the deck down. One by one, ask your helpers to name the card they saw. You will actually FEEL the AMAZEMENT LEVEL rising as each helper shouts out, "Ace of spades!" Will they feel a little sheepish? Sure, because they'll know you somehow pulled the WOOL over their eyes. But that won't stop them from having a BAAAA-LL!

4

PATTER PROMPTER

"You're a great audience, and I sense that we have all bonded a little bit during the show. I want to try an experiment to see just how CLOSE we have become."

7: PUTTING ON A SHOW

PLANNING THE SHOW

It has been said that magic is 10 percent technique and 90 percent performance. In other words, if you don't present a card trick with STYLE and FLAIR, your audience will not be impressed—EVEN IF THE TRICK WORKS PERFECTLY. It's not fair, but hey, that's show-biz. So practice until you know each trick's STORY, STEPS, and SNEAKY STUFF by heart.

Once you've mastered the tricks in this book, you may be tempted to unleash them individually on your little sister, your Uncle Louie, the mailman, or even the family pet. For MAXIMUM EFFECT, however, you need a real, live STAGE SHOW. If you're ready to take this step, then read on. You are about to learn the secrets of TRUE MAGICIANHOOD!

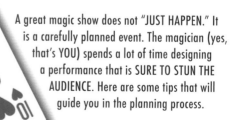

A great magic show does not "JUST HAPPEN." It is a carefully planned event. The magician (yes, that's YOU) spends a lot of time designing a performance that is SURE TO STUN THE AUDIENCE. Here are some tips that will guide you in the planning process.

The KEY TASK in planning a magic show is choosing the tricks you will perform. Please exercise a little self-control here; there is no need to do EVERY TRICK IN THE BOOK. Choose five or six great tricks that use different techniques and flow smoothly from one to the next. Always use the most spectacular trick as your show's GRAND FINALE!

When you've chosen your tricks and the order in which you will do them, PRACTICE THE WHOLE THING. And then PRACTICE AGAIN. And then PRACTICE SOME MORE. Do it in front of a mirror so you will see what the audience sees.

You might even come up with a THEME for your show. Do you want to be a funny magician, or a serious magician, or a dramatic magician? Now is the time to decide.

At some point you will feel like a pro. Now, and ONLY NOW, can you set a date and time for your show and decide who will attend..

PATTER PROMPTER

Make sure you rehearse your patter as well as your moves. THIS IS ESSENTIAL, because the way you deliver your patter can make or break a card trick. THINK ABOUT IT. Imagine a stuttering magician, or one who forgets her lines, or one who does his tricks in utter silence. BOOO-RRRING.

SETTING UP

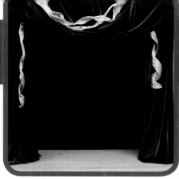

Let's spend a moment thinking about the VENUE (performer-speak for "place") of your magic show. Here are some things to think about when putting together a POLISHED, PROFESSIONAL PRESENTATION.

Gather everything you will need for your show (decks of cards, pencils, paper, coins, etc.). Nothing ruins a trick like MISSING EQUIPMENT!

Consider your LIGHTING NEEDS. A room's regular lights might not create the effect you want. Substitute floor lamps, strings of colorful holiday lights, or anything else you like.

Prepare a STAGE AREA for yourself. Make sure your stage includes a table; you'll need it for most of the tricks in this book. Cover the table with a fancy cloth so it looks OFFICIAL.

Make sure there are enough SEATS for everyone attending your show.

Do you want your audience to see you UP CLOSE, or would you feel more confident if they were a bit farther away? Choose your venue accordingly (small or large).

62

LOOKING THE PART

You've probably noticed that magicians do not usually wear regular clothes. They tend to wear **DRAMATIC DUDS** of some sort. There is a reason for this. A dressed-up magician looks, well, **LIKE A MAGICIAN**. And when you look the part, your audience assumes you know what you're doing. In other words, **THEY TRUST YOU**—and that trust makes your job much easier.

Think about what kind of show you want to put on, then plan your outfit accordingly.

Will you be a **FUNNY MAGICIAN**? If so, you could wear brightly colored clothes made of showy materials. Silky or shiny stuff is always good. You might even consider wearing a clown outfit if you want to be completely comical.

Will you be a **MYSTERIOUS MAGICIAN**? If so, a dark suit or dress is always a good choice. Make sure your stage area and lighting are dark and creepy, too.

Will you be a **TRADITIONAL MAGICIAN**? If so, go with a black top hat and a flowing cape. You can even work a magic wand into your act if you like.

IT'S SHOWTIME!

All your hard work pays off when SHOWTIME arrives. You've planned, arranged, and gotten dressed up. You've done special preparations mentioned in the "Set the Stage" sections of your card tricks. Your PROPS (a word that means "items used in a show") are in place. All that's left is the actual PERFORMANCE. Get out there and give it your best. Or as they say in show business, BREAK A LEG!

BUT WAIT! We're not quite done. We have saved two EXTREMELY IMPORTANT bits of information for last. They are rules that every professional magician lives by—and you must, too, if you want to count yourself among the elite. These rules are:

1. Never reveal your magical secrets.
2. Never repeat a trick, no matter
how much your audience begs.

Why are these rules so important? Simple: Repeating tricks—or even worse, revealing your methods—ruins the mystery. And magicians cannot amaze people who know how their tricks work. So KEEP YOUR MOUTH SHUT. It's not easy, but you're a magician now. You can do it—it's WRITTEN IN THE CARDS!

64